BLACK BEAUTY'S
EARLY DAYS IN THE MEADOW

By ANNA SEWELL ❧ *Illustrated by* JANE MONROE DONOVAN

The first place that I can well
remember was a large pleasant
meadow with a pond of clear
water in it.

Some shady trees leaned over it,
and rushes and water lilies grew
at the deep end.

Over the hedge on one side we looked into a plowed field, and on the other we looked over a gate at our master's house, which stood by the roadside.

At the top of the meadow was a plantation of fir trees, and at the bottom a running brook overhung by a steep bank.

While I was young I lived upon my mother's milk, as I could not eat grass.

In the daytime I ran by her side,

and at night I lay down close by her.

When it was hot we used to stand
by the pond in the shade of the trees,

and when it was cold,
we had a nice warm shed.

As soon as I was old enough to eat grass, my mother
used to go out to work in the daytime,

and come back in the evening.

There were six young colts in the meadow besides me; they were older than I was; some were nearly as large as grown-up horses.

I used to run with them, and had great fun; we used to gallop all together round and round the field, as hard as we could go.

Sometimes we had rather rough play, for they
would frequently bite and kick as well as gallop.

One day, when there was a good deal of kicking, my mother whinnied to me to come to her, and then she said:

"I wish you to pay attention to what I am going to say to you."

"You have been well bred and well born; your father has a great name in these parts, and your grandfather won the cup two years at the Newmarket races.

Your grandmother had the sweetest temper of any horse I ever knew, and I think you have never seen me kick or bite.

I hope you will grow up gentle and good, and never learn bad ways; do your work with a good will, lift your feet up well when you trot, and never bite or kick even in play."

I have never forgotten my mother's advice;
I knew she was a wise old horse, and our
master thought a great deal of her.

To my brother Rick who shares my love of nature and animals.
And to everyone who appreciates the strength and beauty of the horse.

JANE

∽

ILLUSTRATOR'S ACKNOWLEDGMENTS

I would like to express my deepest appreciation to the following people for their help
in either sharing photographs with me or allowing me to photograph their horses:
Marge Paris, Lynn Davidson, and Pamela Vandermolen, owner of Starstruck Arabians.
Their generosity was a great help in making it possible for me to complete this book.

Anna Sewell's *Black Beauty* was first published in 1877.
All new text in this edition is copyright © 2006 by Sleeping Bear Press.

Illustration copyright © 2006 Jane Monroe Donovan

Sleeping Bear Press™

310 North Main Street, Suite 300
Chelsea, MI 48118
www.sleepingbearpress.com

THOMSON
———— ✳ ————™
GALE

© 2006 Thomson Gale, a part of the Thomson Corporation.

Thomson, Star Logo and Sleeping Bear Press are trademarks
and Gale is a registered trademark used herein under license.

Printed and bound in China.

First Edition

10 9 8 7 6 5 4 3 2 1

Library of Congress Cataloging-in-Publication Data on File.